Letter from America

by

Michaela Morgan

Illustrated by Ros Asquith

EAST RENFREWSHIRE COUNCIL	
0505634	
Cypher	06.03.05
M GREEN	£4.99

First published in 2004 in Great Britain by
Barrington Stoke Ltd, Sandeman House, Trunk's Close,
55 High Street, Edinburgh EH1 1SR

Copyright © 2004 Michaela Morgan
Illustrations © Ros Asquith

ISBN 1-842991-85-X

Printed by Polestar Wheatons Ltd

A Note from the Author – Michaela Morgan

Do you ever get any letters? I hardly get any nowadays. I get e-mails of course and text messages and postcards – but real letters are always something special.

So here's a book for all of you who like reading letters – and for those of you who like reading *other people's* letters it's a special treat! I have to admit that I'm a bit of a nosey parker. I get some of my best ideas for stories from watching other people – or listening to them and imagining what it's like to be them.

Stories give you a chance to have a snoop into someone else's life. So turn the page and enter the world of *Tommo* (a bit fed up in London) and *Shelley* (feeling full of life in New York). Enjoy!

To Lindsey

Contents

Chapter 1
Tommo

Rose Galvin School
West 69th Street
New York, New York,
10018 USA

Dear Thomas,

Hi! My name is Shelley Devane. I'm your new pen pal.

Your name was given to me just now in my English class. We've all been given the name of someone to write to in a school in London, England. I have no idea why. It's Miss Carter's idea of a good time. She teaches us English and she just LOVES everything English.

"Write to English kids," she says. "Tell them all about yourself and life here in the USA. It will be FASCINATING!" she says.

So – fascinate me.

AND she says we're all to write regular letters, so we'll need paper, envelopes ... stamps. Has she never HEARD of e-mail!! Or texting?

It makes NO sense. I'm so mad, I've brought my dad's old typewriter to school. It's a protest! I bang away at the keys and every time I do this Miss Carter jumps.

Hee hee. Revenge is sweet!!!

Your new pen pal,

Shelley Devane

Tommo Tomlinson held the thin airmail letter in his hand. His English teacher, Mrs Sadler, had just handed it to him and told him all about her new idea.

He had wanted to sigh and roll his eyes and say "Boring!"

This is what he always did when Mrs Sadler told him another of her ideas. But he couldn't help getting just a bit interested in the thought of someone thousands of miles away writing to him. And a real old-

fashioned letter! He never got real letters.
He got birthday cards, Christmas cards –
but he had NEVER had a proper letter
before. And now here he was with a letter
from the USA in his hand. He'd ripped open
the envelope.

All the other kids had opened their
envelopes too.

Now they were all showing their letters to each other.

"Look at the handwriting! Weird or what?"

"What stamp did *you* get?"

"What does yours say?"

Then they moved on to comparing pen pals.

"Lucky dog!" Mal turned to Tommo. "Yours is a girl!"

Now Tommo sat with his sheet of paper and his pen ready. Mrs Sadler had said this whole lesson was just for them to write their letters.

He'd sat and scratched his head.

Then he'd lost his pen ...

REASONS not to write a letter:

No ink

Empty brain

Pen rolled under Mrs. Sadler's desk

He'd found his pen ...

He'd dropped his pen ...

He'd chewed his pen.

Now there was nothing for it. He'd have to start writing ...

Parkway Comprehensive
Parkway Road
Hammersmith
London
W6 8FB

Dear Shelley,

No one calls me Thomas.

Everyone calls me Tommo. Every week at this time I have to sit here and write a letter to you. What do you want to know? What can I tell you?

My name's Tommo. I'm nearly 14. I like football. I like music. I like having a good time. But I don't like

writing letters. I don't think I've even
written a letter before. Is that
FASCINATING enough for you?

Yours sincerely,

Tommo Tomlinson

Rose Galvin School
West 69th Street
New York, New York,
10018 USA

Dear Tommo,

No, your letter was not fascinating.

You like music. So *give me details*.
What sort of music? Pop music? Rock
music? Hip-hop? Rap? House? Garage?
R and B? Nursery rhymes?

And you like having a good time.
What's a "good time" in England?

Is it standing in the rain getting
wet? Is it walking through the fog
getting lost? Is it drinking cups of tea
and waving little flags at the Queen?

Here are some details about me. I'm
14 (well nearly). I LOVE shopping and

hanging out with my friends. My best friend is called Jade. We share everything together. We share clothes, we share make up, we share secrets. We can talk for HOURS. We talk about everything. Talking is one of my favorite things (but Jade says I'm a good listener, too).

I like music, too. Dance music is my favorite. I love to dance – that's *my* idea of a good time. I love movies, cartoons and TV. I'm SERIOUSLY into kickboxing. Boy can I kick!

Jade has a pen pal too. He's called Tim Spicer. Do you know him? He writes longer letters than you. *And* he sent a photo.

Write back soon. This time add details. Remember I want DETAILS. Information. Hard facts. Don't bother

with details about football. That's
boring.

Yours truly,

Shelley

P.S. I kinda like this old typewriter.
I feel like a cool newshound in one of
those old black and white movies!

Parkway Comprehensive
Parkway Road
Hammersmith
London W6 8FB

Dear Shelley,

Football is not boring but Tim
Spicer is. No wonder he writes long
letters to your friend. He's got nothing
better to do. And that photo he sent? I
bet it isn't him. What do you look like?

So you like shopping? How
FASCINATING.

This letter project is all the idea of
Mrs Sadler or Saddo as we call her.
She's staring at me now. "Are you
writing, Thomas Tomlinson?" she says.
She has a BAD temper.

Now she's glaring at me. She's
getting angry. I need to write

12

something. What can I tell you? OK. Here're 20 things you didn't know about Tommo Tomlinson.

TWENTY FASCINATING FACTS ABOUT ME

1. My favourite team is Manchester United.

2. I like most sorts of music.

3. I don't like dancing.

4. I don't like shopping.

5. My best mates are Gary and Will.

6. I've never got lost in the fog (you've been watching too many old films. London has changed since Jack the Ripper's day).

7. I do not make a habit of standing in the rain.

8. Or drinking tea.

9. I've never waved little flags at the Queen.

10. I like films, videos and the telly too. Comedy and action movies are the best.

11. My favourite colour is black or denim-blue.

12. I've got two sisters (both younger than me, both pests) and one older brother (Terry).

13. I've got a one-eyed cat called Charlie. He lost his eye in a fight. Now he looks like a pirate.

14. Fave foods – hamburgers or beefburgers (what's the difference?) and chips, lots of chips (or french fries to you).

15. I've got a mountain bike. But no mountains to ride on.

16. I do a really good frog sound.

17. I'm pretty good at Donald Duck, too.

18. Most of the time I'm bored.

19. I can't think of any more fascinating facts.

20. I think my mum and dad are going to break up.

That's it. **End of lesson. End of letter**.

Yours sincerely,

Tommo

The bell rang. Tommo stuffed the letter in an envelope, licked it, stuck it down and handed it in. Then he grabbed his bag and was off. Home time.

He was outside the school gates when the thought hit him. Had he really said THAT? Had he really written, "20. I think my mum and dad are going to break up."

What a stupid thing to write – to someone he'd never even met! He thought about going back and trying to get the letter back. But why had he written that anyway? He hadn't even known that he was

thinking it. The words had just floated up
to the top of his head and out onto the
paper. And now that he'd said it, he had a
horrible feeling it might be true.

Back home the telly was blaring. His
little sisters had the cartoons on full
volume. Terry, his older brother, was
playing his music at full-blast and his mum
was huddled in the kitchen on the phone to
one of her friends. She was complaining
about his dad again.

"Honestly, Karen," she was saying, "I just don't know how much longer I can stand it ..."

It seemed that what Tommo had written in his letter was true after all. Until he'd written it, he hadn't even known he'd thought it. Now it was all clear to him. Everything was going to change. And not for the better.

Chapter 2
Shelley

Ten days later in New York, Shelley was sitting on Jade's desk. They were comparing letters and comparing pen pals.

"Tim's letters are way longer than the ones you get," boasted Jade.

"But Tommo's letters are way more FASCINATING!" giggled Shelley. "I think he's cool."

"No way," said Jade. "He seems to think everything's boring. He sounds like a drag."

"He's OK," said Shelley. "He just needs a more positive attitude. I'll work on him."

"Hmm," said Jade. "I'm not so sure ... and look at this number 20 in his so called 'fascinating facts'. What's all that about?"

"Oh, I understand that!" said Shelley. "I'm just the same. I don't know what I'm thinking till I say it. I know exactly how he feels and I'm going to write him a real long letter all about it."

The bell went and Shelley and Jade settled down to do their letter writing.

Rose Galvin School
West 69th Street
New York, New York,
10018 USA

Dear Tommo,

Let me guess how life is at your house. Your mom's on the phone all the time. Am I right? She's always whispering to her friends.

Your dad comes in late. When he comes into the room, she goes out. It's like living in one of those little, wooden weather clock houses, isn't it? When the man with the umbrella comes out, the woman goes in.

I'm right, aren't I?

When you're in bed you can hear them shouting and screaming, hissing at each other. And when you go in a room it all goes quiet and they pretend everything's fine.

Yes? Am I right?

That's how it was in my house anyway. Now my mom and dad have

24

split up and I've got a stepdad. He's OK. I'm OK. You survive. I know, believe me.

Look on the bright side – every holiday and birthday I get two sets of gifts now instead of one. So it's not all bad.

Thanks for your 20 fascinating facts. Here, in return, is the A to Z of me in all my glory. Hey! You could learn from this – have a POSITIVE outlook. Feel good about yourself! Toot your own trumpet! You English have a lot to learn!

The A to Z of Shelley Devane

A – My Ambition is to dance on the stage.

B – I'm Blonde and Beautiful. I'll be all the rage.

C – Cute as a button, that's Shelley Devane.

D – Do you think I'm going insane?

E – Extra Exciting, that's me!

F – And I'm FASCINATING as you'll see.

G – Gee what else can I say?

H – Hey, I'm Happy most of the day.

I – I go Ice skating now and then.

J – Jade's my best friend, my brother's called Ben.

K – I can Kick really high.

L – I've got Long Legs – that's why.

M – **Maximum action – always on the go.**

N – **Am I boring you? No, No, No!**

O – **On top of the world, that's where I'll be.**

P – **Popularity queen, that's me, Shelley!**

Q – **Queen of soul ...**

R – **and Rock 'n Roll.**

S – **A Superstar is what I'll be.**

T – **Trendsetter, go-getter.**

U – **Up to the minute Shelley.**

V – **Victory, that's my aim.**

W - Winning the day and getting fame!

X - eXtra special - do you agree?

Y - Yeah, Yeah! That's Shell-ey.

Hey now I have to fly,

Z - zzzzzz - tired out now - goodbye!

Your friend, the mega-modest superstar,

Shelley

P.S. Since I started using this old typewriter EVERYONE wants one! I'm a real trendsetter!

Shelley folded the letter up and put it in the envelope. On the back of the envelope she wrote in colours,

Don't worry. Be happy.

Then she handed it in.

Chapter 3
Tommo and Shelley

Parkway Comprehensive
Parkway Road
Hammersmith
London W6 8FB

Dear Shelley,

Thanks for your letter. Your A to Z
was a laugh. A bit over the top, isn't it?
Is it supposed to be a rap? I might try

to write one about me but not just yet.
I don't know what to write. That other
stuff you wrote – about my family – it
was spot on. It's funny – you seem to
know my family. They are exactly as
you said. It made me feel better to
know I'm not the only one with
problem parents.

Last night was terrible. Mum said
she was moving out.

"Get your stuff," she said to me.
"We're going to your auntie's."

"You're not leaving," says my dad.
"*I'm* leaving!"

"I'm divorcing you," says Mum.

"No you're not," says my dad. "I'm
divorcing *you*."

I wish I could divorce both of them.

In the end, no one went anywhere.
I was glad about that. I don't want to
go to my auntie's. She's mad. She
always wears a hat. A red one. Whether
she's indoors or outdoors, she's always
wearing her red hat. Maybe she's bald.
I bet she has a bath wearing that hat.

Last year she asked me what I
wanted for my birthday and I told her I
wanted a Manga video. You know the
ones. Japanese cartoon. Rock-hard.
Loads of action. And she agreed to get
it!

"All right," she says, "one Manga
video."

Wow! I couldn't wait to show THAT
to all my mates.

But guess what? What do I find when I unwrap my present from her one week later? A PINGU video!

Do you know what Pingu is?

It's a cartoon about a penguin for little kids.

Pingu can't speak. He squeaks.

He has tiny little adventures in the snow.

My brother fell about laughing at me.

A Pingu video!

I hope we're not leaving home. I hope we're not going to live at my mad auntie's. She might make us all wear red hats and watch Pingu. Write soon before I change into the red-hatted-penguin-monster.

Just as well you write to me at school. I might be at a different address soon.

Best wishes,

Tommo

Rose Galvin School
West 69th Street
New York, New York,
10018 USA

Tommo,

See, I'm not writing "DEAR Tommo"
and do you know why? Because you
ended your letter "Best wishes". I know
we're supposed to be writing regular
letters, not e-mails, but hey, get real!

"Best wishes" is what you write to
someone you hardly know. Why not
write "Love from" or "Your friend" to
me?

Anyway, you're right – I do know
how you feel about your family and,
guess what? I have a mad auntie too!

What is it about aunties – are they ALL mad?

Jade says her aunties are mad too.

Mine does not wear a red hat and I only see her at family parties – weddings, birthdays, thanksgivings. She always says the same thing, "My! How big you are now!" She seems to think I should still be a baby. Every time she comes to my house, my mom gets out all the baby photos of me! AAAAAAGGGGHHH!! Maybe, like you, I'm a bit shy – about some things anyway.

FASCINATING FACTS ABOUT ME WHEN I WAS A BABY:

1. I was a BEAUTIFUL baby!

2. That's if you like bald babies.

3. Bald, gummy babies.

4. Bald, gummy babies with fat faces.

5. Yeah – if that's beautiful then I was BEAUTIFUL.

I will send you a photo of me as I look now – when I get a good one. I do look a lot better than when I was a baby! I've got hair now! I've got *long* hair. And it's blonde – nearly. (Well VERY light brown.) I am no longer gummy! I have lots of teeth. Maybe even a few too many. I'm going to get them fixed soon.

I have eyes (two of them). They're blue (both of them). And I'm tall. Very tall. This is handy for basketball, kickboxing and for getting things down from tall shelves, but bad when you're dancing with a short boy.

How tall are you?

Hope you're not homeless yet. You need a home if you're going to watch your Pingu video. (Did you say it was about a rock-hard, Japanese penguin?!)

Love,

Shelley

163a West Gate,
Hammersmith,
London W6 8JZ

DEAR Shelley,

How's that?

I'm not homeless. I'm writing from
home. I'm not stuck at my mad auntie's
house wearing a red hat. Mum and Dad
have decided to "try again". So I'm still
here. At home with my Pingu video.
And everything is exactly the same
except, instead of shouting at each
other, Mum and Dad just bite their lips.

Fascinating fact ... Did you know
there's a place in Norway called Hell?
Really, there is. I think it must be a bit
like this place.

Mrs Sadler (Saddo to us) told us today that she's leaving to have a baby. (I thought she was looking fatter than usual.) So that means we don't have to go on with this writing to a pen pal stuff unless we want to. What do you think?

I'd sort of like to carry on writing if that's all right with you. I feel like I can talk to you (which is odd as I never have TALKED to you). I'd really have to shout if you were going to hear me in New York - or run up a mega phone bill. But do you know what I mean? Will and Gary are good mates - great mates. Good for a laugh - but I couldn't TALK to them. Do you see what I mean?

Very BEST wishes,

Your pen pal,

Tommo

Rose Galvin School
West 69th Street
New York, New York,
10018 USA

Dear Tommo,

I did NOT know there is a place in
Norway called Hell. But I do know that
there's a place in Sweden called A.
That's true – not a joke. It's a
fascinating fact.

I'm sending you a Christmas card
with this letter. Do you like it? When I
saw a card with penguins on it I had to
get it for you. And when I saw that the
penguins were wearing red hats I just
had to send it to you RIGHT AWAY, even
though it's still only March.

Let's keep writing to each other.
I like getting your letters. It's kind of

fun getting a real envelope to open, and then taking a real letter to the mail. I keep thinking you might send me a photo. Why don't you? And you didn't answer my question about how tall you are. Are you hiding something from me?

If you don't send me a photo I will just think you look like this:

By the way, this is a picture of me:

Ha ha! Fooled you! But I do look a bit like her – same colour eyes (both of them).

OK. I WILL SEND A REAL PHOTO
SOON.

But I haven't got a good one yet.

Write soon. Tell me what you're
going to do in the holidays and tell me
your New Year's resolutions (even
though it is still only March). Mine are:

1. To be on time – or early. (And I
think that writing my New Year's
resolutions in March is a very good
start.)

2. To get a photo sent to you as soon
as I can find one which makes me look
as beautiful as I really am.

3. To stop closing my eyes and
looking like a geek when someone
takes my photo.

4. To carry on writing to you.

5. To become a fascinating personality.

What are yours?

Love,

Shelley

163a West Gate,
Hammersmith
London W6 8JZ

Dear Shelley,

Thank you for the penguins in hats card. I'm sending you a card which is full of fat babies (flying ones, too).

Is THIS what you looked like (only without the wings, of course)?

So that's Christmas sorted – and it's still only March.

Now for New Year – my resolutions are:

1. To carry on writing to you.

2. To watch my Pingu video.

3. Then to sell it.

4. To sell ALL the stuff I don't want or need and to start saving money.

5. To leave home. That's what I'm going to use the saved-up money for. I can't wait to get away from here.

Best wishes,

Your friend,

Tommo

163a West Gate,
Hammersmith,
London W6 8JZ.

Dear Shelley,

I know it's not my turn to write. But it's the middle of the night and I HAVE TO TALK TO SOMEBODY so I'm writing to you.

Mum and Dad have just had a row – more like a war really. The things they said ... and I didn't do anything to stop them. I just stayed up here and kept quiet – very quiet. Now Mum has gone. She slammed out of the house. She says she's never coming back.

I should have stopped her. I should have said something, but I didn't know what to do.

Dad is downstairs. I think he's drinking. I don't know what to do. I can't talk to my sisters – they're too little. My brother went off to share a flat with his mate last week. He said he couldn't stand it here. I can't talk to my friends. Things keep going round in my head and I don't know what to do. I hope you don't mind me writing to you like this.

Please write soon,

Tommo

P.S. I'm sorry to write like this. It's not funny or happy or amusing or fascinating.

Sorry.

Apartment 19
303 West 73rd Street,
New York, New York,
10018 USA

Dear Tommo,

I just got your letter and I'm writing
back right away. Don't be sorry. I'm
glad you felt you could write to me. I'm
a friend. And I'm a friend who knows
what it's like. I feel for you. I know
what you're going through. I understand
it.

You don't know what to do. You feel
bad. You think you should have said
something. You think you should have
done something. You think if only you
had done something or been different,
things would have been different. You
feel as if it's all your fault.

It isn't your fault and it isn't up to you to do or say anything. It's up to your mom and dad.

Think about it. If you have a fight with Gary or Will, is it your mom's fault? No. Did she make it happen? No. Is there anything she could say or do that will make it all better? No. It would be up to you and Will and Gary to deal with it.

That's what it's like with your mom and dad. It's up to THEM to deal with it or not deal with it. Sure, you can listen to them or talk to them or help out in small ways, but it's not up to you to sort it out for them and IT IS NOT YOUR FAULT.

So, you don't know what to do – and the answer is you don't do anything. You carry on as best you can. You go to school. You go out with your friends. You don't spend all your time thinking about it. Believe me, I KNOW. I worked it all out over the last two years.

Most of all you do not do anything like running away. It'll only make it worse. Much, much worse.

At least you now have food, a bed, friends around you and you're safe. No matter how bad it gets at home, it is worse on the run, out on the streets. Now, OK I don't KNOW this for sure – 'cos I've never done it – but you only have to watch the news once or twice to get some idea of how bad it can get out there. There are maniacs and madmen out there. It's cold. You're too young to get a job. You'd be hungry. You'd be in danger. So stay where you are.

DO NOT RUN AWAY!

Things *will* get better. You just have to hang on in there. I hope this helps. Write whenever you like. Don't use your savings to run away – hey, you might need them one day to come visit me! You'd have to sell a whole bunch of penguin videos to pay for that though!

Love,

Your friend,

Shelley

Tommo held the letter in his hand. All over the envelope Shelley had written URGENT! URGENT! and on the back she'd put her usual message:

Don't worry. Be happy.

Well, he wasn't happy. But he did feel a whole lot better. Things didn't seem so bad after a while and one thing was for sure – it was good to have a friend to write to. Shelley had turned out to be a great friend. He was going to find a card to send to tell her that. Maybe this writing to pen pals wasn't such a bad idea after all.

He looked through the racks of cards. Now if only he could find one with a penguin on ...

Then he saw it.

The world is a warmer place with you.
It's good to have a friend.

Two penguins huddled on an iceberg.

Under the picture it said:

The world is a warmer place with you.

It's good to have a friend.

He picked it up. His face felt hot and
red. What if Will or Gary saw him sending a

card like that? They had stopped writing to their pen pals weeks ago. They would think he was soft. Then he stood up and boldly walked to the counter and gave it to the girl on the till. She looked at it as she put it in a bag. She smiled. "I love penguins," she said. "I think they're great."

Tommo smiled back. "So do I," he said.

Barrington Stoke would like to thank all its readers for commenting on the manuscript before publication and in particular:

Johnny Anderson
Heather Armitage
Iain Barnard
Elizabeth Bodkin
Ciaran Brown
Rachel Brown
Declan Cameron
Chris Cooper
Megan Corsie
Liam Deeny
Nicola Dickson
Harriet Earp
Denise Ferguson
Sophie Ferguson
Mrs Gripper
Ryan Harkin
Scott Hastings
David Hefferland
Chloe Horsfield
Natalie Hynd

Leo Johnson
Verity Kent
Kiera Kingsman
Cameron McKinlay
Lauren McNair
George Pincher
William Potter
Leanne Richards
Jonathan Riordan
Abby Robertson
Lauren Scott
Amy Smith
Mrs Smith
Eileen Spiers
Archie Stewart
Saowalak Thomson
Holly Tobin
Samantha Tyler
Brogan White
Alison Wood

Become a Consultant!

Would you like to give us feedback on our titles before they are published? Contact us at the address or website below – we'd love to hear from you!

Barrington Stoke, Sandeman House, Trunk's Close,
55 High Street, Edinburgh EH1 1SR
Tel: 0131 557 2020 Fax: 0131 557 6060
E-mail: info@barringtonstoke.co.uk
Website: www.barringtonstoke.co.uk